Walt Disney Presents

Winnie-the-Pooh

MEETS GOPHER

Based on a story by A. A. Milne

Pictures by
THE WALT DISNEY STUDIO

Adapted by
GEORGE DESANTIS

GOLDEN PRESS · NEW YORK

*W*innie–the–Pooh lived in the forest under the name
Sanders, which means he had the name Sanders over
the door and he lived *under* it.

One day when Pooh was sitting resting his clock chimed.

"Now what does that mean?" wondered Pooh.

He knew it meant something, but being a bear of little brain, he had to think and think.

Ah yes, that was it. It was time for his stoutness exercises. Up-down, up-down went Pooh, humming a little hum.

Doing his stoutness exercises always made Pooh
hungry.

Oh bother. The honey pot was empty again. There
was nothing in it. He would have to go out and find some.

And so Pooh went out walking and he came to a sandy bank with a hole in it. It was Rabbit's hole. And Rabbit might say, "What about a bit of lunch?"

"Is anybody at home?" called Pooh.

"NO!" said a voice.

"Bother," said Pooh. "Isn't that you, Rabbit?"

"NO!" said the voice.

Pooh stuck his head in the hole.

"Oh hello, Pooh," said Rabbit. "What a pleasant surprise. What about a bit of lunch?"

"I *do* feel like a little something, now that I come to think of it," said Pooh. And he settled down to a large small helping of honey and condensed milk (without the bread).

For a long time Pooh ate and ate and ate.

Then, in rather a sticky voice, he said good-bye to Rabbit and started to climb out of the hole.

"Oh help. Oh bother. I'm stuck," said Pooh.

"It all comes of eating too much," said Rabbit, and he started pushing. But it was no help.

"It all comes from not having front doors big enough," said Pooh.

"I shall go and fetch Christopher Robin," said Rabbit, dashing out of the back door. "Don't go away."

"I say, are you stuck?" said Owl, who had landed nearby.

"No, I'm just resting and thinking," said Pooh.

Owl looked at him closely. "You, sir, are stuck," he said. "This situation obviously calls for an expert."

"Here I am," said Samuel J. Gopher. "An excavation expert, at your service."

Gopher strutted around Pooh, poking and prodding.

"Hmm...hard digging...danger of a cave-in...need planks for bracing...big job...two or three days..."

"Two or three days?" said Pooh. "What about lunches?"

"No problem," said Gopher. "Always bring my own lunch. Run into money....strictly cash...think it over... let me know...here's my card."

And he disappeared as suddenly as he had come.

"Cheer up, Pooh Bear, we're coming," called a voice. Christopher Robin and Kanga and Roo and Piglet and Eeyore and Rabbit appeared over the hill. They started pulling and pulling.

"There's only one thing to do," said Christopher Robin, at last. "We'll have to wait until you get thin."

"Might take weeks. Or even months," said Eeyore sadly.

"And no meals," said Christopher Robin.

And so there was Winnie the Pooh, half in and half out of Rabbit's hole.

Night fell and rain fell, and when Pooh got wet Rabbit and the others had to wring him out.

They sang him Sustaining Songs and tried to cheer him up, and Pooh tried not to think of eating.

Then they all went home and Pooh was left alone. "I still think I could blast you out of there," said Gopher, appearing suddenly. "You *are* that stuck-up bear, aren't you?" he added.

"Yes," said Pooh absently, eying Gopher's lunch box.

"What's in that box?" said Pooh, suspecting something.

"Let me see," said Gopher busily, "there's a little cold
salmon and some custard and ah—oh yes, some honey—"

"Honey?" breathed Pooh.

"Honey?" gasped Rabbit, inside his hole. "Oh no! Not that!"

Finding his front door still full he dashed out by the back door and ran around just in time to see....

…Gopher politely handing Pooh a fat jar of honey.

"Stop it at once," said Rabbit, snatching away the jar. "Not one drop."

"But Rabbit, I wasn't going to eat it," said Pooh in an offended tone of voice. "Only taste it."

"*I* will taste it," Rabbit said grandly. "*You* are in a pre-dicament. No tasting. No eating. Till you are thin."

Thoughtfully he tasted the honey, then gave the jar back to Gopher. "Very good. In fact, not bad at all. But not for Pooh Bear."

Rabbit was quite busy for a long time, down in his hole.

When he came up he had a sign which he had made. The sign said,

DON'T FEED THE BEAR

Gopher didn't come back after that.

Pooh got thinner and thinner until at last, when they all pulled, and Rabbit pushed, POP! out came Pooh, and off he went flying through the air.

Christopher Robin and Piglet and Eeyore and Kanga and Roo all landed in a heap.

"Where is he?" said Rabbit looking out from his front door at last.

"Stuck again," said Eeyore sadly.

"Don't worry, silly old bear," said Christopher Robin in a loving voice. "We'll get you out."

"There's no hurry," mumbled Pooh Bear. "This is the right kind of tree and the right kind of bee."

What a happy ending for Pooh!